Upside Down
Harry Brown

Written by Martin Waddell
Illustrated by Annabel Spenceley

'I wish that I was upside down!'
said Harry Brown, and . . .

Harry Brown was upside down.

Harry Brown put on his clothes,
but Harry did it
upside down!

Harry Brown went down the stairs,
but Harry did it
upside down.

Harry went off to town,
but Harry did it
upside down.

'Harry Brown, Upside Down!'
the school kids cried.
The kids were the right way up,
not like Harry Brown.
Harry Brown was upside down!

Harry sat down on his chair,
but he did it
upside down.

Harry did maths

and played football

and had his dinner . . .
upside down!

The man from TV came to see
Upside Down Harry Brown.

The Head sent for Harry's mum.
She told her that she had to come.

'Stop standing on your head!' Mum said.
But Harry couldn't stop it!

Mum took Harry home to bed.
Harry got in . . .
upside down.

'I wish that I was right way up!'
Harry said next morning, and . . .

Upside Down Harry Brown
was the right way up! But . . .

'I wish that I could fly!' said Harry,
and . . .

19

Harry Brown flew around his room.

22

Harry Brown flew off to town.

24